Military Tech

MILITARY SHIPS

JULIA GARSTECKI

BLACK
RABBIT
BOOKS

Bolt is published by Black Rabbit Books
P.O. Box 3263, Mankato, Minnesota, 56002.
www.blackrabbitbooks.com
Copyright © 2018 Black Rabbit Books

Marysa Storm, editor; Michael Sellner, designer;
Omay Ayres, photo researcher

Library of Congress Cataloging-in-Publication Data
Names: Garstecki, Julia, author.
Title: Military ships / by Julia Garstecki.
Description: Mankato, Minnesota : Black Rabbit Books, [2018] | Series: Bolt.
Military tech | Includes bibliographical references and index. | Audience:
Grades 4-6. | Audience: Ages 9-12.
Identifiers: LCCN 2016049972 (print) | LCCN 2016050335 (ebook) | ISBN
9781680721669 (library binding) | ISBN 9781680722307 (e-book)
Subjects: LCSH: Warships–Juvenile literature.
Classification: LCC V765 .G37 2018 (print) | LCC V765 (ebook) | DDC
623.825–dc23
LC record available at https://lccn.loc.gov/2016049972

Printed in the United States at CG Book Printers,
North Mankato, Minnesota, 56003. 3/17

CONTENTS

CHAPTER 1

Watercraft in ACTION

The water looks calm. It seems like just another day. Suddenly, a **missile** breaks the surface. With a flash, it shoots into the sky.

The weapon came from a submarine. The sub is deep underwater. Few people know it's there.

Navies use ships and subs. Some ships carry aircraft. Others attack. Subs go on secret missions.

Ships AND SUBS

AMPHIBIOUS ASSAULT VEHICLES
MOVE SOLDIERS TO LAND

AIRCRAFT CARRIERS
MOVE AIRCRAFT

DESTROYERS
FIGHT ALONE OR IN GROUPS

SUBS
CARRY OUT SECRET MISSIONS

CHAPTER 2

Aircraft
CARRIERS

Carriers rule the oceans. They are the largest **warships**. They move aircraft closer to battles. These ships have runways. Planes can take off and land on them.

Liaoning is a Chinese carrier. It has a ski jump deck. The end of the deck curves up. The curve directs planes up and forward. It makes taking off easier.

SKI JUMP
DECK

FORD-CLASS
By the Numbers

AROUND
34.5
MILES
(56 kilometers)
PER HOUR

SPEED OF
FORD-CLASS
CARRIER

MORE THAN 75
NUMBER OF AIRCRAFT IT CAN CARRY

Ford-Class Carriers

There's a new group of U.S. carriers. It is the Ford-class. Most carriers use steam to help planes take off. These ships use electric energy. Electric energy is easier to control than steam. Launches will be smoother.

1,092 FEET
(333 METERS)
length of
Ford-class carrier

AROUND
4,500
CREW MEMBERS

Nimitz-Class Carriers

The U.S. Navy also has Nimitz-class carriers. These carriers have a 50-year life span. They go more than 20 years without refueling. Jets can launch from the ships every 20 seconds.

Carriers are like floating cities. The ships even have their own post offices onboard.

PARTS OF A CARRIER

RUNWAYS

CATAPULTS

FLIGHT DECK

ISLAND

HULL

CHAPTER 3

SUBMARINES

Subs carry soldiers on secret missions. They are also built to attack. They fire weapons at ships. They go after other subs too.

The HMS *Artful* is from the United Kingdom. It is one of the **Royal Navy's** most powerful subs. It can hit targets around 746 miles (1,200 km) away. The targets can be in water or on land.

K-329 Severodvinsk

The *K-329 Severodvinsk* is a Russian sub. It is especially **stealthy**. Part of it is coated with a material that **absorbs** sound. The sub cannot be heard underwater. It has lots of weapons too. Its enemies won't know what hit them.

It took more than 20 years to make the *K-329*.

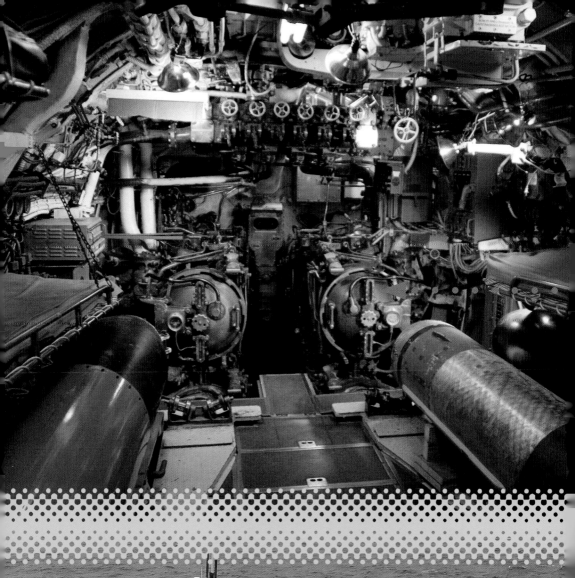

Seawolf subs cost a lot. The United States planned to have 12 made. But the subs became too expensive. Only three were built.

Seawolf-Class Submarines

Seawolf is a U.S. class of subs. The subs are extremely quiet. They are deadly too. The subs weren't just made to hunt enemies. They were built to destroy them. The subs have eight **torpedo** tubes. They can also carry missiles.

Maximum Diving Depth

0	
500	
1,000	**HMS ARTFUL** ASTUTE-CLASS
1,500	more than 984 feet (300 m)
2,000	USS *JIMMY CARTER* SEAWOLF-CLASS · K-329 *SEVERODVINSK* YASEN-CLASS
2,500	around 2,000 feet (610 m)

Top Speed Underwater

HMS ARTFUL

USS *JIMMY CARTER*

K-329 *SEVERODVINSK*

10   15

Length

318 feet (97 m)

HMS ARTFUL

450 feet (137 m)

USS JIMMY CARTER

390.4 feet (119 m)

K-329 SEVERODVINSK

100 150 200 250 300 350 400 450

35 miles (56 km) **per hour**

46 miles (74 km) **per hour**

40 miles (64 km) **per hour**

20   25   30   35   40   45

CHAPTER 4

Destroyers and Amphibious Assault VEHICLES

Military boats are battle ready too. Amphibious Assault Vehicles (AAVs) can attack. Destroyers are built to fight.

AAVs work on land and in water. They travel from ship to shore. The AAV7A1 carries supplies and soldiers. The vehicle is heavily **armored**. It also has weapons. Soldiers inside are kept safe.

AAV7A1's Speeds on Water and Land

LAND SPEED	45 miles (72 km) per hour	
WATER SPEED	8 miles (13 km) per hour	

0   10   20   30   40   50

JS *Izumo*

The JS *Izumo* is a Japanese helicopter destroyer. It acts a lot like an aircraft carrier. It can hold 14 helicopters. It carries troops and trucks too. The ship also holds extra fuel. It can refuel other boats.

USS *Zumwalt*

The USS *Zumwalt* is a huge destroyer. It is 610 feet (186 m) long. But it looks much smaller on **radar**. On radar, it looks like a 50-foot (15-m) boat. Its strange shape confuses radar.

There are many kinds of ships and subs. They do different jobs. Some move soldiers. Others carry aircraft. They are all powerful military tools.

GLOSSARY

absorb (ub-ZORB)—to take in

amphibious (am-FIB-ee-uhs)—able to work on both land and water

armored (AHR-merd)—covered in flat pieces of metal used for protection

catapult (KAT-uh-puhlt)—a device for launching an airplane from the deck of a ship

missile (MIS-uhl)—something that can be thrown or projected to hit an object far away

radar (RAY-dar)—a device that sends out radio waves for finding the location and speed of a moving object

Royal Navy (ROI-uhl NEY-vee)—the United Kingdom's navy

stealthy (STEL-thee)—quiet and secret in order to avoid being noticed

torpedo (tawr-PEE-doh)—a bomb shaped like a tube that is fired underwater

warship (WAWR-ship)—a military ship built for combat

BOOKS

Arnold, Quinn M. *Nimitz Aircraft Carrier.* Now That's Big! Mankato, MN: Creative Education, 2016.

Harasymiw, Mark. *Life on a Submarine.* Extreme Jobs in Extreme Places. New York: Gareth Stevens Pub., 2013.

Marsico, Katie. *Warships.* A True Book. New York: Children's Press, an imprint of Scholastic Inc., 2016.

WEBSITES

Facts About Submarines
www.scienceforkidsclub.com/submarines.html

United States Armed Forces
**www.ducksters.com/history/us_government/
united_states_armed_forces.php**

U.S. Navy Ships
www.navy.mil/navydata/our_ships.asp

INDEX